For Trent

My dearest son,
in a very natural way, your boundless energy and magical curiosity put me in the right
place at the right time. It was your need to explore a chaotic world and make sense of it,
and my need to be the best parent I could, which created Humphrey.
Humphrey has taught us both. And that gives meaning to his character. It makes me
happy to know that when we are apart, you are safe within your own heart.

I love you
Mom   C. N.

Copyright © 1999 by Nord-Süd Verlag AG, Gossau Zürich, Switzerland
First published in Switzerland under the title *Das schönste Weihnachtsgeschenk*

First published in the United States, Great Britain, Canada, Australia,
and New Zealand in 1999 by North-South Books,
an imprint of Nord-Süd Verlag AG, Gossau Zürich, Switzerland

Distributed in the United States by North-South Books Inc., New York.

Library of Congress Cataloging-in-Publication Data is available.
A CIP catalogue record for this book is available from The British Library.

ISBN O-7358-1145-8 (trade binding) 10 9 8 7 6 5 4 3 2 1
ISBN O-7358-1146-6 (library binding) 10 9 8 7 6 5 4 3 2 1

Printed in Belgium

For more information about our books, and the authors and artists
who create them, visit our web site: http://www.northsouth.com

CHARISE NEUGEBAUER

SANTA'S GIFT

ILLUSTRATED BY
BARBARA NASCIMBENI

A MICHAEL
NEUGEBAUER
BOOK

NORTH-SOUTH BOOKS

NEW YORK/LONDON

Someone was knocking on Humphrey's door.
He rubbed his eyes and tried to wake up.

It was Timothy.
He needed Humphrey to read a letter.

Humphrey was surprised
that Timothy had received a letter.
Timothy never shared his toys,
so he didn't have any friends.
Except for Humphrey.
Humphrey loved everyone.
And everyone loved him.

Humphrey looked at it closely.
The letter was from Santa!

Dear Timothy,

   I received your Christmas wish list. But there is a problem. I haven't found a new toy that's fast enough, big enough, or bright enough to keep you happy for a whole year.
   So I must tell you that I won't be visiting you this year.
   I wish you a Merry Christmas.

                              Love from
                              Santa Claus

Timothy began to cry.
New toys were the only thing he cared about.
But this year Santa wasn't coming.

Humphrey offered to help Timothy write a letter to Santa.

Dear Santa Claus,

There has been a terrible misunderstanding. I love new toys. It doesn't matter what it is. If it's a new toy, I'll love it! Please, please, please bring me a new toy for Christmas! I promise I'll be happy. I promise I'll play with it until next Christmas. Please, please, please.

Best wishes,
Timothy

Soon Timothy received another letter from the North Pole. He ran to Humphrey's house.

Dear Timothy,

I will leave a Christmas surprise for you.
Please remember that only you can make the fun
last until I visit you again next year.

Love from
Santa Claus

Timothy jumped up and down after hearing the good news!
He spent the entire day waiting, wondering, and imagining
what special new toy Santa would leave for him.

On Christmas morning Timothy raced to the Christmas tree. *run*
Wow! There were presents everywhere!
Timothy ran to open the biggest one first. He looked at the tag.
It didn't look like his name. Timothy checked the next one.
Then the next. *shocked sad face*
"Oh, no! Santa delivered these presents to the wrong house.
Someone else has my new toy!" cried Timothy.

Humphrey stopped by to see what special toy Santa had delivered.

Between sobs, Timothy explained the mix-up.
Humphrey just couldn't believe it.
He'd never heard of Santa making a mistake.

Then Humphrey spotted a note attached to the Christmas tree.

Dear Timothy,

The thing I enjoy most throughout the year is the joy of giving. So, this is the Christmas gift I give to you. I hope you enjoy delivering my gifts as much as I do. Merry Christmas!

Love from
Santa Claus

This was unbelievable.
Santa had left more new toys than Timothy could count.
And none of them was for him. Not one! angry, cross arms

"Well," said Humphrey. "If we're going to deliver all these, look toward T, wide open arms
we'd better get started."

"Are you crazy? I'm not going to deliver them. Nobody even likes me!"

crossed arms, turn away from It

Humphrey left Timothy in front of the tree crying. *power walk*
He went straight home and started to work.
Soon he hung his invitation in the middle of town.

hammer

Then Humphrey hurried back to Timothy's to get everything ready.

There was a knock at the door.
"Who could that be?" asked Timothy.
He opened the door.
"Merry Christmas!" they all shouted.

"Welcome to our Christmas party!" Humphrey said, inviting his friends in.

"What's going on?" asked Timothy, surprised.

"It's Christmas!" answered Humphrey excitedly.
He began calling out the names on the gifts.
"Melanie, Melinda, Johnny and Karen!
Janie and Linda, Ronnie and Darrin!"
Everyone smiled happily at Humphrey
as he gave them their gifts.
Everyone, except Timothy.

"Thank you! I love it!
It's my first brand-new toy!"
They jumped and they laughed.
And they shouted with joy!

It really was a great
Christmas party,
thought Timothy.

Then something surprising happened.
"Hey Humphrey, stop! This is *my* gift from Santa!"
exclaimed Timothy. "He wanted *me* to deliver his toys!"

With Humphrey's help, Timothy proudly handed out Santa's gifts.

hand out

"A tea set for Jessica. For Maria a doll.
A skateboard. A scooter. Be careful. Don't fall.
A train set for Joey.
For Ben a new ball.
I'm glad that you're here.
Merry Christmas to all!"

Everyone had a wonderful time.
Andy was the last guest to leave. He turned to Timothy.
"Would you like to play with us tomorrow?"

Timothy's face lit up like a Christmas tree. "Yes!" he shouted happily.
"I'd love to!"

Later there was a knock at the door.

But when Timothy opened it:
No one was there. *Confused*
Then he saw the letter.